PENELOPE'S PENDANT

PENELOPE'S PENDANT

DOUGLAS HILL

ILLUSTRATED BY STEVE JOHNSON

DOUBLEDAY
NEW YORK   LONDON   TORONTO   SYDNEY   AUCKLAND

All of the characters in this book are fictitious, and
any resemblance to actual persons, living or dead,
is purely coincidental.

DESIGNED BY PETER R. KRUZAN

PUBLISHED BY DOUBLEDAY
a division of Bantam Doubleday Dell Publishing Group, Inc.
666 Fifth Avenue, New York, New York 10103

DOUBLEDAY
and the portrayal of an anchor with a dolphin
are trademarks of Doubleday, a division of
Bantam Doubleday Dell Publishing Group, Inc.

Library of Congress Cataloging-in-Publication Data

Hill, Douglas Arthur, 1935–
Penelope's pendant / Douglas Hill.—1st ed. in the United States
of America.
p.   cm.
Summary: Eleven-year-old Penny finds a slightly damaged
pendant on the beach and discovers that it gives her the
power to move herself and other objects through space.
[1. Magic—Fiction.   2. Humorous stories.]   I. Title.
PZ7.H5493Pe   1991
[Fic]—dc20   90-34866   CIP   AC

ISBN 0-385-41641-5

FOR ELLEN
a Penny for your thoughts

PENELOPE'S
PENDANT

1

A GLEAM
IN THE SAND

Penny came upon the shiny thing during a Sunday at the seaside, when she wandered away from the family picnic on the beach. Pretending to be a beachcomber, she was gazing down at the sand, searching for interesting stones, shells and other treasures. She spotted the dull gleam half-buried beneath a flat rock and thought it was the lid of a tin or the bottom of a broken milk bottle.

She poked it with a bare toe, picked it up, and saw that it was some kind of pendant.

It wasn't much to look at. A disc of vaguely silvery metal, thicker in the middle than at the edges, covered in scratches and dents. But Penny liked the weight of it in her hand, and the way the dents and scratches seemed almost to make a pattern. Also, she was impressed by the way the thin silvery chain seemed weirdly to *grow* out of the pendant, without any kind of link or fastening that she could see.

She slipped the chain over her head and looked down, enjoying the way the pendant hung solidly against her shirt. In fact, she thought, finding the pendant was just about the most enjoyable thing that had happened all day.

It was supposed to have been a nice day out by the sea, but it had not been a great success. Her brother Alan—who was fourteen, three years older than Penny—hadn't wanted to go at all, claiming that beaches and picnics were boring. So he had sulked for much of the time and picked on Penny even more than usual.

Also, the weather had been unkind—cool and cloudy with a stiff breeze off the sea. Alan had huddled in his jacket and made a great many sour remarks about icebergs and polar bears, which had annoyed their mother. Then Penny had dropped her sandwich in the sand, which had annoyed their mother even more—though it had made Alan laugh nastily and had delighted all the insects that had come uninvited to the picnic.

But now Penny's beachcombing had turned up a treasure. Of course she didn't think for a moment that the pendant could be valuable. Not

when it was just plain metal, covered with dents and scratches. But it was interesting, and she liked it. And if it wasn't valuable, there would be no problem if she kept it.

She looked back along the beach toward her family. They were all doing exactly what she knew they would be doing. Her brother had his Walkman earplugs in place and was lost in a private world of sound. Her father was reading his newspaper, an activity that he could drag out through a whole day if he wanted to. And her mother was putting the picnic things away, looking a little tight-lipped because no one was helping her.

Penny also knew exactly what would happen if she took the pendant to show them. Her brother would laugh at it and mock her. Her father would look up vaguely and say something like "mmm." And her mother would smile briefly, barely glance at the pendant, and then tell Penny to help with the clearing up.

All the same, Penny thought, she had found a kind of treasure, and she wanted to show *some*-one. So she ran lightly over the sand toward the family group.

"Look what I found!" she cried as she bounced up to the picnic blanket that was spread on the sand, holding out her hand with the pendant.

Her brother pulled one earplug aside and

looked at it, then laughed loudly. "What an ugly piece of junk!" he jeered.

Her father looked up from his paper, blinking vaguely. "Mmm," he said.

And her mother smiled faintly, barely glancing at the pendant. "Give me a hand with these things," she told Penny, "before you do *any*thing else."

Sighing, Penny slipped the pendant's chain back over her head and knelt to gather up some of the picnic things. First of all, she started gathering the small plastic glasses that had held their soft drinks.

She began with the glasses because she was feeling a bit thirsty and she had seen that her brother's glass was still half full. But even with both earplugs back in place, Alan wasn't missing anything.

"Leave that! I haven't finished!" he snapped, as Penny reached across the blanket for his glass.

She drew back with another sigh and cleared up some other things. And naturally, as always happens, she began to feel even more thirsty— just because there was nothing else left to drink.

"Alan," she finally pleaded, "can I have just a sip of your drink?"

He stared at her coldly, then shook his head no.

"Please?" she begged.

To her surprise, he smiled. But then the smile became a mocking grin, as he pulled his earplugs away once more.

"I'll swap you," he said through his grin. "You can have a sip—a *little* sip—if you give me that piece of junk you found."

Penny put a protective hand around her pendant. She was thirsty, she thought, but not *that* thirsty. She knew that Alan would try to smash the pendant, or throw it away, or do something to it to upset her.

"No," she said. "I'm keeping it."

"Fine," Alan said loftily, putting his earplugs back in. "No drink, then. But you're probably right to keep the thing. It's so ugly—it suits you perfectly."

"Stop it, you two," their mother said. "Penny, put those things in the hamper."

Penny began to turn away, gritting her teeth with anger at her brother's last remark. But then she turned back, startled.

Her brother had given a sharp yelp of dismay and had made a desperate lunge forward.

He was too late. The plastic glass holding what was left of his drink tilted and toppled over, to make a sticky puddle on the blanket.

At once their mother was mopping it up with a handful of tissues, at the same time scolding

6

Alan for his clumsiness and carelessness and reminding him how he could try to be some help rather than making more work. Alan was trying to interrupt with complaints about how the glass just fell over and he didn't touch it and it wasn't his fault. Even their father had lowered his newspaper to gaze at the scene with vague disapproval.

Normally Penny would have joined in, getting her own back with some laughter and mockery at Alan's expense. But for once she remained silent. She was totally astonished.

In that fleeting instant when Alan had yelped and lunged, something had seemed to happen that *couldn't* have happened.

Penny had seen Alan's glass—eerily and weirdly, all by itself—*lift up* an inch or so from the blanket. And then, just before it tipped over, she had seen it begin, impossibly, to *float* an inch or so through the air toward her.

2

ANOTHER
IMPOSSIBLE THING

Penny was amazed that no one else had noticed the weird movement of Alan's drink before it spilled. At the same time, she knew better than to say anything about what *she* had seen. She would be accused of "seeing things" or making up silly stories—even though she was absolutely sure that she had seen an impossible thing happen.

Instead, she remained quiet and thoughtful through the rest of the clearing up—and all through the drive back to the smallish inland town where she and her family lived.

Later that night, alone in her cozy little room, supposedly getting ready for bed, Penny stood silently looking at herself in the mirror. She saw what she always saw—a slim girl, nearly eleven years old, average height, short brown hair, heart-shaped face, brown eyes. Nothing remarkable or unusual. She thought of herself as being plain and ordinary, even though her father often called her "pretty Penny." That was only him being a father—just as Alan was only being a brother when he sometimes called her "Penny dreadful." (Her mother just called her Penny, except for the times when she was annoyed and called her "PenELope" in *that* tone of voice.)

But for once, that night, her mirror image did have something remarkable and unusual about it—the silvery disc of metal that was hanging, from its strange chain, against her shirt.

Two odd and special things had happened that day, Penny thought. She had found the pendant—and Alan's drink had moved in an impossible way.

Could there somehow be a *connection* between the two things?

But then her mother called upstairs, with the usual bedtime urgings toward pajamas and toothbrushes. That led Penny into a high-speed dash to get to the bathroom just before Alan. Shortly afterward, she was in her pajamas and climbing into bed. She was still wearing the pendant—but wearing it inside her pajamas, so her mother wouldn't see it and tell her to take it off.

I'm going to wear it all the time from now on, she told herself. And we'll see if any more impossible things happen.

A moment later, after her mother had looked in to say goodnight, Penny was reaching drowsily over to turn off her bedside lamp. But then she hesitated, feeling her heart sink. She had noticed, on her bedside table, a cassette tape.

It was a tape by her very favorite rock group. Unfortunately, the group was also one of Alan's favorites. And it was Alan's tape—which Penny had "borrowed" (without asking) that morning.

She flicked off the light and lay back, feeling very lucky that Alan hadn't yet noticed the missing tape. First thing in the morning, she told herself, she would sneak into Alan's room—when he was out of it—and put the tape back.

She settled down to sleep, still thinking of the tape and how quick and stealthy she would have to be to return it unseen. And as her eyes closed, and all those thoughts swirled around in her mind, she had the strangest feeling.

Inside her pajamas the pendant's comfortable weight was resting on her bare skin. And in that moment it suddenly became quite a lot warmer, and made her skin tingle faintly where it touched.

Started back to wakefulness, Penny sat up

quickly, turned on her light, and lifted the pendant out to look at it. But it looked just the same. And by then the strange feelings, the tingling and the warmth, had faded and vanished.

Penny frowned for a moment, wondering if the feelings had been part of a going-to-sleep dream. Then she wondered if perhaps she should take the pendant off, after all. But in the end she left it on—*out*side her pajamas. Yawning, she reached over to turn off the light again.

She was too sleepy, and thinking too much about the pendant, to notice the really peculiar thing that had happened.

And in the morning, when her mother looked in to wake her, Penny was too dozy at first to notice.

It wasn't until she had got washed and was getting dressed that she noticed.

She heard her brother thunder down the stairs—"doing his herd of elephants act," as their mother always said—toward breakfast. Knowing that his room was empty and the coast was clear, Penny turned to pick up the cassette tape that she had to return.

But the tape wasn't there.

She knew that she hadn't moved it. A quick search of the floor around the table and under the bed showed that it hadn't fallen off. She couldn't find it anywhere.

Had Alan come in quietly and taken the tape, she wondered, while she was asleep? She doubted it. Alan would more likely have woken her up and gone on at her for taking the tape in the first place.

But then where had it gone?

Slowly her hand crept up to touch the pendant, while a small chill slid along her spine. Maybe the warmth and tingling from the pendant in the night *hadn't* been a dream.

The pendant had behaved strangely. Now, just as strangely, the cassette tape was gone.

Quietly, nervously, Penny slipped along the hall to her brother's room. His things were in their usual heaps and messes, but she had no trouble finding what she was looking for.

The tape that had been on her bedside table was now lying on top of a pile of other tapes, on Alan's chest of drawers.

Feeling even more chilled and nervous, she went back to her own room. On the way, her mother called from downstairs.

"Penny! Breakfast!"

"Coming!" Penny called back, in a shaky voice that didn't sound like hers at all.

In her room, she glanced into the mirror and saw that she looked almost as pale and shaky as she felt—and as frightened.

For she was just about as sure as she could be that this new impossible thing, with the tape, had something—everything—to do with the pendant.

Yet she wasn't afraid of the pendant itself. It was too scruffy and beat-up to be scary. Something else was frightening her. Some kind of . . . power.

But Penny had her fair share of courage, and perhaps more than her share of curiosity. Despite her fears, she badly wanted to know what the power was and how it worked. *If* it worked.

She reached up with a slightly trembling hand and took hold of the pendant. Her grip was so tight that her knuckles went white. Then she thought—as clearly and firmly as she could— about the cassette tape that had moved so mysteriously from her room to her brother's. As she thought about the tape, she also thought about how she would like to have it back in her room. How she *needed* it back in her room.

The thoughts gathered in her mind—just as similar thoughts about the tape had gathered the night before. As they did so, the pendant in her hand turned suddenly warmer, and her palm and fingers tingled where they gripped it.

With a small shriek, Penny opened her hand

13

and let the pendant fall against her shirt. Then her legs went weak and she almost fell herself.

Something flat and shiny zipped past her, through the air, like a flash of light.

And a cassette tape dropped with a clatter onto the top of her bedside table.

Penny took several moments to find the courage and the strength to move over to the table. Then she peered warily down at the tape that had somehow, by itself, arrived in her room.

It seemed even *more* disturbing—though Penny wasn't sure why—when she saw that the tape on her table was an old one by a group that had been out of fashion and out of action for about two years.

Whatever the pendant's power was, however it worked, it had brought her the wrong tape.

3

A DAY OF MAGIC

It was nothing more than pure habit that got Penny downstairs to the breakfast table. Along with the fact, perhaps, that her mother had started to call "PenELope" in *that* tone of voice. At the table, Penny had no real idea what she was doing, or saying, or eating. But she must have been doing fairly normal things—out of habit—because no one paid her much attention.

Her father had already left for work, with his newspaper. Her mother was rushing around getting ready to leave for *her* work. And Alan, whose turn it was to wash up the breakfast dishes, was doing so with as much grumbling and splashing as he thought he could get away with.

Penny knew that if she had really looked peculiar in any way, her mother would have noticed. But in fact Penny wasn't feeling, or looking, pale and shaky any longer. If anything, she was starting to feel a bit flushed—with total dazed astonishment, and also with a dawning excitement.

Yes, it was scary. But it was also wonderful. Though she knew it was impossible and couldn't happen, it somehow was true and was happening.

The strange, scruffy disc of metal hanging from her neck was a *magic* pendant.

As the excitement and delight grew within her, more strongly than any doubt or fear, she knew for certain that she was going to keep on wearing the pendant, all the time.

She had a small moment of panic as she gathered up her books and things in the front hall. Alan, doing the same thing next to her, glanced at her and then burst into scornful laughter.

"You're not wearing that piece of junk to *school,* are you?" he said, pointing at the pendant.

Penny looked quickly at their mother. But their mother was more concerned with what her watch was saying.

"Come on, come *on,* we'll be *late,*" she said, and swept the two of them out of the house with her.

There they went separate ways. Alan had to catch a bus to his secondary school, but Penny usually walked—or ran, when it rained—the shorter distance to her school. On the way, just as usual, she met her closest friend, Tish.

Tish—for Letitia—was small, slightly plump, very pretty, and a month older than Penny. She had a mass of curly blond hair and large hazel eyes that mostly wore a faraway dreamy look behind round glasses. But despite glasses and dreaminess, Tish's eyes seldom missed a thing. They certainly didn't miss the strange disc hanging from Penny's neck.

"What's *that*?" Tish demanded. "Where'd you get it?" She reached out, grasped the pendant, and peered at it. "Did it cost much? I mean— It's not really very *pretty,* or anything . . ."

Her voice trailed away as she finally saw the look on Penny's face. A look that showed all the mixture of amazement, excitement, fear and doubt that was churning around inside Penny.

"Tish," Penny said in a low voice, "I have a secret to tell you. But you have to promise . . ."

"I won't tell *anyone*?" Tish said breathlessly, almost jumping up and down. "What is it?"

"I found this pendant yesterday," Penny said. "And I found out . . . that it has secret magical powers."

For a long moment Tish stared at Penny, hazel eyes wide. Then she exploded into a stream of high-pitched, shrieking giggles.

Scowling, Penny turned and walked away. In a moment Tish caught up with her, trying to get her giggles under control.

"That was so *funny,*" she gasped. "That bashed-up old thing being *magic* . . ."

Penny said nothing, but merely walked on, still scowling. Except that she also took the pendant and slid it down under her loose-fitting pullover, out of sight.

"Wouldn't it be *lovely,* though!" Tish was saying, not noticing Penny's scowl. "To have magic power . . . You know what *I'd* like? I'd like to have the power to turn invisible! Then I could go round and *watch* people—see what they get up to when they think no one's looking . . ."

Penny turned, her scowl changing into a shocked expression. "Tish! You *wouldn't* . . ."

But then she closed her mouth firmly. She certainly wasn't going to get into a long discussion with Tish about magic powers and what to do with them. Not when Tish clearly didn't believe in such things for a moment.

That was when Penny realized that she wasn't going to be able to talk about the pendant to anyone. Not her friends, not her parents, no one. Because she knew that no one would ever believe her.

So she became very quiet and thoughtful again, while Tish chattered happily the rest of their way to school. And she stayed quiet and thoughtful through the hubbub of the school-yard, and then into the school and the classroom.

She was thinking about keeping her pendant a secret, and about what various people might say and do if they knew the truth. But most of all she was thinking about the pendant itself, and its power—and wondering what the power really could do, or could *not* do.

She already had a bit of an idea about the power. And she began to get more of an idea during that day when more impossible things started to happen.

The first impossible thing of the day happened when Penny realized that she had left a particular textbook at home, and that the teacher was just about to tell the class to take out that book and open it. It was a desperate situation, so Penny decided to try to use the pendant.

She didn't think she had to touch it or hold it, since it had seemed to work before when it was just hanging round her neck. So she simply made a silent plea. In her mind, without speaking, she said: *Please bring me my book.*

Through her shirt, faintly, she felt the pendant's sudden tingling warmth.

And the book arrived.

But it didn't come to her hand or onto her desk. It appeared high in the air, near the ceiling, unseen by everyone in the classroom—including Penny, at first. Penny had no idea that it had arrived until it fell all the way down to the floor, landing beside her desk with a loud *splat*.

"Clumsy!" That was Tish, laughing at her from the seat next to hers. Several other children had turned to look, because of the noise. But because they had all been taking *their* books out, they hadn't noticed anything. As far as they knew, Penny had simply dropped a book.

"Are you having some difficulty, Penny?" the teacher said, with a sour look in Penny's direction.

"No," Penny said quickly, picking up her book. Then she sat back with a small smile, feeling relieved. The book had come to her, and—unlike the cassette tape that she had "called"—it was the right book. So it seemed that the pendant *would* magically do what she wished.

But there was still a lot of nervousness mixed in with her delight. Partly because it was hard to get used to the idea that magic could be *real*, and not something that happened only in fairy tales and fantasy stories.

And more of her nervousness came from the fact that the pendant's magic didn't always seem to work exactly as it should.

Penny got another glimpse of the pendant's unreliability when she and Tish and everyone else were queuing up for school dinner. It was a normal Monday dinner—which meant tasteless gray meat, overcooked vegetables and mashed potatoes. But with it all came nice thick brown gravy, which the children enjoyed because it gave a little flavor to the other things on their plates.

When it came to be Penny's turn to receive her plateful, she saw that the lady serving the gravy was ladling out very small, mean, stingy dollops. Without stopping to think, Penny asked the pendant to give her a little more.

Whereupon, as the pendant warmed and tingled, the entire panful of gravy turned itself over and dumped its contents on Penny's plate.

It was a small Niagara Falls of gravy. With a shriek, Penny dropped her overflowing plate—which added to the mess as the gravy poured over the serving counter and cascaded onto the floor. Other girls around Penny shrieked as well, jumping back from the sticky brown deluge. And the lady who had been serving the gravy shrieked loudest of all.

"It just turned *over!*" she cried. "*I* didn't do *any*thing! The pan just flopped over all by *itself!*"

She was led away, sobbing, by some teachers and other dinner ladies, who all looked slightly amused.

Shortly Penny was given another plateful of food and all was calm again. And she stayed unusually quiet all through dinnertime, with the same small smile on her lips.

Then there was the fourth impossible thing of the day, which was both the most exciting and the most frightening.

It happened in the local library, where Penny had gone after school to return a book and borrow another. While there, she also wanted to look at a special book, for a class project she was doing. But the special book—a big, expensive book with many pictures—was with a lot of other big, expensive books, safe on a very high shelf. Only the librarian was allowed to take those books from the shelf, using a set of steps from behind the library desk.

But Penny saw that the librarian was busy, chatting to some other readers. So, once again, Penny asked the pendant to help.

Afterward, Penny came to realize that she must have somehow made the request too vague in her mind. For the pendant's power didn't bring the book down to her. It took *her* to the book.

It was like an unseen lift beneath her feet, hoisting her off the floor. She floated up toward that top shelf, too startled to make a sound.

But when she reached the shelf, with the book

23

in front of her, the power suddenly *stopped*—as if it had shut itself off.

Penny just had time to clutch at the top shelf with her hands and to scrabble with her feet onto a lower shelf. And she was clinging there like a monkey, shaken and frightened, when the librarian looked over and saw her.

The peaceful silence of the library was shattered as the librarian stormed over to Penny, screeching and scolding as Penny clambered slowly down.

"How *dare* you?" the librarian raged, red-faced. "*Climbing,* on the *shelves*! Where do you think you *are*?"

And on she went, and on, while Penny mumbled apologies and avoided saying what had actually happened.

In the end, Penny was banished from the library, without her book, and banned for a whole month. But while that was bad, she thought, it might have been worse. Besides, she had something else to think about that wasn't bad at all.

It was astonishing enough that the pendant's magic had seemed to move things when she wanted them moved. Moving *herself* was quite another thing.

Yet it had happened. For those few seconds, in the library, she and the pendant had actually . . . sort of . . . *flown.*

4

DARK INTRUDER

Through the rest of that day, and through a very normal evening at home with her family, Penny's excitement and delight began to die down a little. Thoughts of how she might be able to soar around the sky, like Supergirl or something, gave way to more sensible notions. And with them came a return of nervousness.

She began to remember what else had happened in the library.

The power had lifted her into the air. But then, also, it had suddenly *shut off*.

When Penny finally started remembering how *that* had felt, she also started thinking about what might have happened if the power had shut off and just left her in midair, nowhere near any shelves to grab onto.

Or if the power had wafted her out of an upper-story window, instead, and *then* shut off.

So that night, once again in her room getting ready for bed, she made a promise to herself. The promise was that she would be very, very careful about using the pendant's power from then on. She would use it only when she was alone, and safe—when neither she nor anyone else could be hurt if the power went wrong. As it often seemed to do.

That way, she thought, she would learn more about using the pendant—get better at it. In time, she hoped, she would learn to control the power properly, so it wouldn't go wrong.

It was only then that a particular thought struck her for the first time.

The thought had taken a while to come to her because Penny was a quite straightforward, honest girl. She knew the differences between right and wrong and mostly tried to stay away from wrongdoing, even of the more petty sort. She had been startled when her friend Tish had talked of being invisible and spying on people. But even then it had taken Penny some time to realize how many *other* unpleasant, dishonest things might be done with a magical pendant.

Like playing cruel tricks on people who annoyed her. Like cheating at games, by magically moving a ball or something. Like stealing—by telling the pendant to bring her things out of shops and so on, anything she wanted. Like . . . all sorts of things.

But Penny knew herself fairly well. So she knew that if she ever used the pendant to do any of those things—especially things like cheating and stealing—she would feel guilty and miserable and disgusted with herself afterward. So, as she turned out the light that night, she made a second promise to herself.

Not only would she use the pendant carefully and sensibly, she would also be sure never to use it dishonestly.

With the promises made, Penny was able at last to overcome her excitement and settle down to sleep. But in the middle of the night she had a strange dream. Or what certainly seemed like a dream.

In it, she felt herself become partly awake. Light from a streetlamp, and perhaps from the moon, was seeping past her curtains, so she was able to see, dimly.

She saw that there was someone in her room.

As in many dreams, she felt frozen, unable to move or speak. She could only watch as the dim shape of the intruder moved around. He, or it, was a dark gray shadow, short and broad and a little hunched, or maybe crouching. It looked as if he was wearing a long, shapeless coat or cloak, with a hood. And he kept moving jerkily from one place to another in her room, almost as if . . .

. . . As if he was looking for something.

But then he seemed to become alarmed. Perhaps Penny had moved, under her bedclothes. Perhaps she had moaned, or whimpered, with fright. In any case the intruder swung round and looked at her, so that Penny could see the faint glitter of his eyes.

Then he simply vanished.

That was what made Penny so sure that she was dreaming. The way the intruder had disappeared—just winking out, as if his image had somehow been erased.

And also, the way that his shape and size hadn't really seemed . . . normal.

It took Penny a long while to get back to sleep. Then it seemed almost at once that it was time to get up and ready for school. But she was slower than usual to get ready that morning. A cold, clammy feeling had spread along her spine— because she could no longer be sure she had been dreaming during the night.

Her clothes seemed to have been moved in her wardrobe, and objects seemed to have been shifted on top of her dresser.

As if by someone looking for something.

The clammy feeling, and her nervousness generally, kept Penny from thinking too much that day about the pendant and its power. Besides, she was determined to keep her promise to herself about using the pendant only in private, sensibly and carefully.

So the pendant nestled unused, all day long, under Penny's pullover. No books fell, no gravy spilled, no one flew up to high shelves. Nothing peculiar happened at all.

Not until the middle of the following night—when Penny had the dream again.

It was just as before. The dim light, the oddly hunched and shadowy figure moving here and there, even pulling out some of the drawers in Penny's dresser and peering in. And, as before, when he realized that Penny had awakened, the figure vanished into nothing.

But in the morning Penny became quite sure, beyond any doubt, that she had *not* been dreaming.

The drawers of her dresser were not properly shut. And she *knew* that they had been shut the night before.

All that day the cold, clammy feeling was back, and Penny's mind was in a turmoil. Now that she knew the intruder was *real*, not a dream, she was terrified.

She was also sure that she could guess what the shadowy visitor was looking for.

On the third night, when she was awakened by the intruder, Penny found the courage from somewhere to lift her head up and say, shakily, "Who . . . who's there?"

The intruder vanished at once, without even turning around. That made Penny feel a little better. It seemed to show that the intruder was as frightened of her as she was of him. Maybe, she thought, he'll be frightened off altogether.

But he wasn't. He was back the next night, as before, searching and rummaging—and vanishing as soon as he knew Penny was awake.

All the fear and loss of sleep started to have an effect on Penny. Instead of being her usual bright and lively self, she became dull, listless, half awake. Her mother often grew annoyed with her for never listening to anything anyone said. Her teacher often grew annoyed with her, too, for not paying attention. Tish and her other friends grew annoyed with her for never seeming to want to *do* anything.

But Penny couldn't help it. All she could think of was the shadowy figure who was invading her room. And what the intruder was probably looking for. And what he might do, in the end, if he kept failing to find what he wanted.

Even worse, Penny had to deal with it all by herself. She didn't think for a minute that anyone would believe a story about a shadowy being searching her room and vanishing into thin air.

Besides, she didn't feel able to face the teasing from her brother if he heard the story. She remembered all too well how Alan had mocked her when she was little and had wanted a nightlight in her room. She had now outgrown the night-light, but she didn't want to risk having Alan think that she was still afraid of the dark.

Because it wasn't the dark she feared. It was what came into her room *with* the dark.

She even thought that she might take the pendant off, at night, and leave it in plain sight. She was sure that the pendant was what the intruder was looking for. If he was given it, she thought, he might go away for good.

But in the end she couldn't bring herself to do it. It was *her* pendant, she said to herself stubbornly. She didn't want to lose it even to get rid of the intruder. So she kept the pendant around her neck, and clung to the hope that the intruder would eventually get tired of his nighttime searches, and give up.

And if that wasn't enough, at about the same time Penny found another, quite different, reason for being very frightened.

The other reason was a boy named Ralph.

Ralph was a year ahead of Penny at school, but two years older. He was bigger and stronger than any other child in the school. He was also thuggish, mean-minded and violent, always in trouble for fighting, bullying and disrupting lessons. And, along with the small gang of boys that he led, he was often suspected of small crimes, including vandalism.

Penny was usually careful to stay out of Ralph's way, at school or anywhere. But during those days of being tired and frightened, she wasn't always paying much attention to things around her. Walking home from school one day, by herself, she didn't notice the group of boys until she had come right up to them.

Then the noise they made drew her attention. She saw that it was Ralph with his three main followers. There was tall, lanky Errol and a tubby boy whose very small teeth caused him to be called Gummy, and a shorter, stocky boy named Tony. The four of them were clustered around a public telephone.

And the noise that had attracted Penny's attention was the sound of excited voices and the *screech* of twisted metal.

"You got it!" Errol was shouting.

"That's it!" Tony was shouting.

"Ow!" Gummy was shouting—because big Ralph had stepped on his foot.

And Ralph, with a short, hooked iron bar in his hands, which he was using to pry open the telephone cash box, was shouting, "Get outta my *way*, you berk!"

Then there was the crunch and snap of metal being broken, a cheer, and a jangling cascade of coins onto the pavement. And it wasn't until the four boys began to gather up their booty that they saw Penny.

Ralph turned toward her, the iron pry-bar gripped in one hand. The others crowded behind him, glowering. Penny took a step back, then another, poised for flight.

"You saw, didn't you?" Ralph growled.

Penny said nothing, but took another step back. As she did so, all four took a menacing step forward.

"She could get us into trouble, Ralph," Gummy said.

"We got to keep her from tellin', Ralph," Errol said.

Ralph didn't have a chance to reply. Across the street a tall man walked briskly around the corner—then slowed, staring across at the group of children.

The four boys rushed away toward a side

street. But just before they were out of sight, Ralph turned back, waving the iron bar and glaring at Penny.

"You keep your mouth shut," he shouted, "or we'll *get* you!"

5

FEARFUL
DAYS AND NIGHTS

By the time Penny reached home, after that threat, she was feeling even more anxious and shaky. And it must have shown on her face.

"Are you feeling all right, love?" her mother asked. "You're looking pale . . ."

"She's not going to kick the *bucket*, she just looks a little *pail*!" Alan chanted, grinning.

That caused their mother to turn away and have a word with Alan about being both rude and silly. During that, Penny mumbled something about feeling all right and slipped away to her room.

It was strange, she thought, how peaceful her room looked with the light on—and how frightening it could be in the middle of the night, with a prowler in it. But she tried hard to push that thought out of her mind. Once again, as she had been doing for several days, she settled down to a quiet session of practice—with the pendant.

She had been keeping her promise to herself, and not trying anything ambitious or risky. Just *little* magics, moving small objects from here to there. She was so used to the tingling warmth by then that she hardly noticed it anymore. Also, she had learned quite a bit about the pendant's power.

Most importantly, she had learned that the power was useless for many kinds of things. Absolutely nothing happened when she tried to use the pendant for some of the sorts of magic that could be found in stories. She couldn't make things appear out of nothing, or vanish into nothing, the way Aladdin's genie could. She couldn't turn something into something else, the way various wicked witches could.

In fact, the pendant's magic didn't seem able to do *anything* except move things from one place to another. Including Penny herself.

Penny wasn't too disappointed to find that the pendant's magic had its limits. But she *was* disappointed when she found, almost all the time, that the magic didn't work properly.

She was sure that it was her fault—that she

still didn't know enough, or wasn't skilled enough, to use the magic in the right way. Yet no matter how often she practiced, things didn't get any better.

When she tried to move something around, in her room, there was a good chance that it would be the *wrong* thing that moved—as with the cassette tape, before. Or the thing would be moved to the wrong place, as with her school-book. Or other things would be moved as well, as with the flood of gravy.

And Penny was being very, *very* careful about moving herself. Not only because of what had happened in the library, but also because of one time in her room when she had called on the pendant to lift her from the floor to her bed. Instead, she had been swept upward far too quickly and far too far, and had hit her head on the ceiling hard enough to make her see stars.

Even so, Penny kept trying with all the courage and determination—and stubbornness— that she could find in herself. It was *her* magic pendant, and she had to make it work. And for the same reason she kept wearing it all the time, day and night—because it was *hers*, and she wanted to keep it safe from everyone, including shadowy beings who came to search her room.

She often wished that there was a way she

could use the pendant to drive away the night-time intruder. Not to mention using it to protect herself against Ralph. But she didn't think she could do it, so she didn't try. And so she went on being frightened most of the time for the next few days and nights. Which meant that she went on feeling tired and anxious, and looking pale and miserable.

By then no one was being annoyed at her any-more. Instead, her parents, teachers and friends were growing very worried. Her mother was worried enough to march her off to the doctor for a checkup. But the doctor, a brisk and busy man, found nothing wrong.

"Probably growing too fast," the doctor said briskly. "Give her a tonic for a while, see how it goes."

And he busily wrote out a prescription for a sour-tasting liquid that Penny had to take every night, though it clearly did no good at all.

So everyone went on worrying about her. But no matter how often people asked her what was wrong, she was unable to tell them. It was bad enough, she kept thinking, that they were all fussing about her being *ill*. If she told them about magic pendants and shadowy beings that appeared and disappeared in her room, they would all think she was *crazy*.

She did confide in someone, however, about

one of her troubles. That was because several times at school she had run into big Ralph and his gang. She had the sense to be never too far away from a teacher, so the thugs could do nothing *to* her. But they were able to glare and scowl and make threatening gestures, and snarl warnings about how she should remember what she had been told.

When she finally decided to confide in someone about *that* problem, she turned—oddly enough—to her brother Alan. She thought Alan might be old enough to offer useful advice, while still being young enough to take the threat seriously, which an adult might not do.

She half expected Alan simply to laugh at her. But he seemed to be stunned into silence by the very fact that she was telling him her troubles. And he seemed to lose his sense of humor entirely when he had heard her story.

"What d'you expect *me* to do?" Alan asked uneasily, when she was finished.

Despite her misery, Penny had to smile. Her brother may have been fourteen, but he wasn't very tall and he was a bit weedy. He wouldn't be likely to rush off heroically to defend her against big Ralph and that loutish gang.

"I don't expect you to do anything," she said. "I just don't know what *I* should do. I saw them doing a *crime,* Alan. I keep thinking I should tell somebody—but if I do, Ralph and that lot will *kill* me!"

Alan nodded slowly and self-importantly. He looked as if he was quite enjoying being the wise big brother, helping his little sister to know what to do.

"You want to stay well away from all of them," he said at last.

"I know *that!*" Penny said exasperatedly. "But don't you think it's wrong not to tell anyone about a crime?"

"No, not really," Alan said, sounding a bit put out. "It's stupid to put yourself in danger. You don't need to get involved. Before long, that Ralph will do something *really* stupid, and the cops will catch him, and that'll be that. You have nothing to worry about."

"Oh, fine," Penny muttered, and went away, realizing that Alan was not going to be a lot of help.

What do I do in the meantime? she asked herself miserably as she got ready for bed that night. What if Ralph never does get caught?

And what if the prowler gets tired of searching, one night, and . . . *does* something?

And what if . . .

Her troubles seemed to swell and loom and press down upon her like a huge thunderous cloud. A coldness trailed along her spine, a tightness clutched at her throat. That night she came close to leaving her bedside lamp on, and close to sobbing herself to sleep. But in the end she clung to a few scraps of her courage, and did neither.

And in the middle of that night she woke up with a jolt—to find that the prowler *had*, at last, got tired of searching and *had* decided to do something.

He was no longer across the room, but much closer to her bed. And he didn't disappear when Penny woke. She could see him more clearly than ever before—and she desperately wished that she couldn't.

The intruder was a being like nothing she had ever seen, outside of nightmares. He was about Penny's height, stooped and round-shouldered, with a broad body, short legs and long arms. The skin of his face and hands was grayish-white, wrinkled and hairless. The rest of him was covered by a rumpled tunic and high boots under his hooded cloak. He had a small mouth, a long nose, sorrowful-looking eyes—and huge ears that came to sharp points on the upper tips.

And this impossible, horrible creature was standing at the foot of Penny's bed, scowling at her.

6

GLUMDOLE

"You're *wearing* it, aren't you?" the creature said in a breathy, high-pitched voice.

Penny just stared, hardly daring to breathe. Very slowly she reached over with her left hand and pinched her right arm, hard. It hurt quite a lot, and she stopped at once. And the intruder still stood there.

"This is *not* a dream," he said crossly. "Now come along . . ." He reached out with a narrow hand.

Penny dived under the bedclothes. Huddled there, shaking, she tried to cry out but could manage only a tiny, terrified squeak. She curled into a ball and told herself that it had to be a dream, that such things didn't exist, that it would be all right.

"Come *out*," she heard the creature say, even more crossly. "I'm not going to hurt you."

To Penny's horror, the bedclothes began to move downward. She grabbed them but could not stop them. She tried to slide down with them, but met the foot of the bed with a bump. So she lay still, wide-eyed and trembling, as the bed-clothes slid away.

"Trolls' teeth," the creature said. "You'd think I was going to *eat* you."

It wasn't the best choice of words. Penny's trembling grew worse, and she whimpered once, very faintly.

The creature sighed, a deep sad sound. "I suppose I can't blame you. I always think that the few people who *can* see me won't be afraid when they *do* see me. But I'm almost always wrong." He sighed again.

Penny stared, and shook.

"But you needn't be afraid," the creature went on. "I'm no enemy to humans. I'm just an ordinary, peaceful cobold who . . ." He stopped, frowning down at Penny. "You *do* know what a cobold is, don't you?"

Very slowly, Penny moved her head the smallest bit from side to side, to say no.

The creature sighed again. "So much has

gone, all forgotten . . ." He gazed quietly at the floor for a moment, looking so sad that Penny found herself feeling a little less afraid of him—and almost sorry for him.

Then he looked at her again. "Perhaps you've heard of gnomes? Elves? Folk like that?"

Penny slowly moved her head the tiniest bit up and down, to say yes.

"Good!" The creature sounded pleased, though he did not smile. His pinched little mouth didn't look as if it had ever smiled. "Cobolds are related to those sorts of folk, one way or another. And I'm a cobold, from under the hills west of here. Glumdole."

Penny blinked.

"That's my *name*," the creature said, frowning again. "Glumdole. I'm giving you my name so you'll know I won't hurt you. Now you give me yours."

Penny swallowed twice. "Penelope," she said, in the smallest voice she had ever used. It seemed proper to give her full name—and again the creature, the cobold, seemed pleased.

"Good," he said. "Penelope and Glumdole. Very nice. And that means we now have a *name-tie,* binding us together. So you can stop being afraid, and help me. I'm looking for something that used to belong to me, and I think you've been wearing it all this time."

45

Penny swallowed again. "The pendant," she said in her very small voice.

"Correct," said Glumdole. "It's been lost for an age or two, and I'd forgotten all about it. But then under my hills I could feel its power, when you began using it. So I came to find it."

"To take it back?" Penny asked. Through her fear she began to feel quite upset at the thought of giving up the pendant, even if the cobold was its rightful owner.

But Glumdole surprised her. "Not exactly," he said. "I made it as a gift for someone, so the magic couldn't let it belong to me again. Besides, it's yours now, since you found it."

Then he saw the puzzled look in Penny's eyes. With a sigh, shuffling his feet a bit, he explained.

A long time earlier, he said—"even before the great King Arthur"—Glumdole had made the pendant as a special favor for a prince. The prince, named Flubris, had then ruled the area where Penny's town now stood. He was a very rich, spoiled and greedy prince who had grown enormously fat and lazy, and who therefore found it difficult to move around. But he also found it boring to have to call servants all the time, to move him or to fetch things for him.

So he asked Glumdole for some magic that could carry him around and move things for him.

And Glumdole made the pendant for him, as a gift.

"Humans and the Magic Folk got on well together, in those days," Glumdole told Penny. "A few small upsets now and then, mostly over dragons and treasure, but nothing serious. Nowadays, though . . ." He sighed deeply. "No one believes in magic anymore, and the Magic Folk keep themselves to themselves, hidden away. Not that most humans today could see us even if we showed ourselves . . ."

Anyway, Glumdole went on, a time came when an evil lord from another country invaded the lands of the fat and lazy Flubris. The evil lord easily won all the battles, overran Flubris's palace (catching him asleep), looted the palace of all its treasure, including the pendant, and sailed away. And in the years that followed, Prince Flubris became very thin and miserable as well as very poor, and was never able to be lazy again.

"And I thought the pendant was lost forever," Glumdole went on, "for I never again felt its magic being used in the world. Until now. May I see it?"

Slowly Penny pulled the pendant out from under her pajama top and held it up. Glumdole peered at it, frowning and nodding.

"I might have known," he said. "You see those little dents and pits in it? Those held *jewels* when the pendant was new. Emeralds, sapphires, one or two rubies. The thieves must have pulled the jewels out and thrown the pendant away, not knowing what it was."

Penny stared at the pendant, trying to imagine it gleaming with jewels. She thought of where she had found it, at the seaside—probably just where the evil lord's men had tossed it, before they sailed away.

"That's why the power felt *strange* to me," Glumdole was saying, "when you began using it. Some of the magic was in the jewels. It isn't working properly now, is it?"

"Not really," Penelope whispered.

Glumdole nodded. "Then I see that I was right to come and find it."

"What . . . what will you do to it?" Penny asked in her small voice.

"I can't *fix* it, if that's what you're thinking," Glumdole said. "Once a magic goes out of order, it stays that way. You'll never be able to make it do exactly what you want. Things will always go wrong. You could hurt yourself with it, or do some damage." He sighed another deep sigh. "I expect I'll have to destroy it. If you'll just let me have it . . ."

But Penny, with the pendant in her hand, did

not move. Glumdole had only told her what she already understood—that the pendant could be dangerous. But, she thought, nothing had gone seriously wrong yet. She had used the pendant many times without being really hurt or causing any real damage. Nothing more than a little bang on the head, some spilled gravy . . .

And she still felt that it was *her* pendant, *her* magic. In fact Glumdole had said that very thing. It was hers because she had found it. Finders keepers.

"Do you . . . really *have* to destroy it?" she whispered.

Glumdole looked surprised. "Well, no—not as if there's a *law*. I just meant that I *should* destroy it, because it could be harmful. But 'should' isn't 'must,' as people say."

"Then . . ." Penny gathered her courage. "Then could I keep it?"

Glumdole stared at her. Then he frowned, and sighed, and shuffled his feet. "I might have known. *Humans.* Never can resist magic, you people, when you believe in it. Whatever the dangers." He sighed again. "If you want to keep it, Penelope, I can't stop you. It belongs to you, now."

Penny smiled, suddenly realizing that she was no longer the slightest bit afraid of Glumdole. "Then I *will* keep it. Thank you."

Glumdole sighed more deeply than ever. "If you must. But never forget the danger, Penelope. Try not to use it for anything too grand, or too important. That way, if the magic goes wrong, it won't be serious." He paused, shuffled his feet, frowned. "And if you ever change your mind, or get into trouble with it . . . well, remember that we have a name-tie, you and I."

As he spoke the word "I" he seemed to twitch one pointed ear—and vanished, as suddenly as he had all the other times.

7

DIRE THREATS

Penny hardly slept at all for the rest of the night. But for the first time in a long while she didn't feel the least bit tired or troubled. As the dawn turned into morning, and her room brightened with the rise of the sun, she lay looking up at her ceiling with a delighted smile.

She was happy enough to know that she would never again need to be afraid of a nighttime prowler. But that was only a part of her delight. Mostly, she was thrilled to know that she held a very special secret.

"There *is* such a thing as magic," she whispered to herself. "There *are* magical beings. I've met one of the beings—and I own a piece of magic."

She pulled the pendant out and held it up, gazing at it admiringly. "I don't care if you don't have jewels anymore," she whispered. "I think you're marvelous. And you belong to me."

Beyond her room she heard her parents moving around, beginning the day. Slowly she got out of bed, pausing briefly to look at herself and the pendant in the mirror. It seemed a terrible letdown to do ordinary things like going to school after the wonderful thing that had happened in the night. She knew she wouldn't be able to pay proper attention.

And there was another problem. She was dying to *tell* someone about meeting Glumdole, to share her amazing secret. But she knew she couldn't—remembering when she had told Tish, her best friend, about the pendant. If she now talked about Glumdole she certainly wouldn't be believed, and people would think she was getting really weird.

Then another troubling thought struck her. It might be worse if someone *did* believe her. Because, she realized, just about everyone would want a magic pendant if they knew such a thing truly existed. Unpleasant people might even try to take it away from her. Or the government and important people like that would make her give it up.

So she looked at herself in the mirror and

made an even stronger promise to herself—a vow—that she would never tell another soul about the pendant. Ever.

Then she grinned at her mirror image and began to get dressed.

At the breakfast table she was still smiling her small private smile. Her father smiled back at her and said it was nice to see her looking happy. Her mother looked at her curiously and asked if she was all right. And her brother peered at her suspiciously and demanded to know what she was grinning at.

Once again Penny felt the terrible urge to tell them about the wonderful thing that had happened. The urge was so strong that she began to worry. If she kept her secret bottled up inside her, it might spill out sometime before she could stop it—maybe at the worst possible time.

Then she realized: if there was anyone in the world she *could* tell, it was her family. They wouldn't believe her, of course. But her parents wouldn't even really pay much attention. And Alan would laugh, but Alan always laughed at her. So she could get rid of her bursting need to tell someone, without any risk.

"I'm feeling good this morning," she announced. "In the night a magical being came to my room and talked to me. He seemed a bit sad, in a way, but he was very nice, and kind."

Penny felt better at once. The bursting, dying-to-tell feeling was gone. And, she saw, her family had received her news exactly as she expected. Her father just said "mmm" as he turned a page of his newspaper. Her mother smiled vaguely and fondly at what she clearly thought was a flight of childish imagination. And her brother was laughing with loud and heavy mockery.

"Baby dreams!" he jeered. "Fairies and pixies coming to visit!"

"He isn't a fairy or a pixie," Penny said calmly. "He's a cobold." And she poured milk over her cereal and began to eat.

Her parents, she saw, were no longer listening. As for Alan, he had been briefly silenced by the word "cobold." Clearly, he hadn't the faintest idea what it meant.

"Cobold cobblers," he muttered, looking annoyed. Penny ignored him. Their mother then drew Alan's attention to the time, and the value of eating rather than talking. Alan quieted down and began to shovel cereal into his mouth. And Penny smiled her private smile and felt very good indeed.

But the feeling didn't last even up to the school gate, because on the way to school Tish produced news that made Penny feel as if her insides had started growing icicles.

"It's Ralph!" Tish said excitedly. "The *police* went round to his house after school yesterday! Asking a lot of questions—saying he was suspected of being a *vandal* and things! They said they'd be *watching* him, and he could get into trouble . . . And Ralph's father gave him a belting, after!"

Penny felt cold and sick. "How do you know all this?" she asked weakly.

Tish's hazel eyes, behind her glasses, were bright with the joy of gossip. "Ralph's mother told her neighbor, who told a friend of my mum. So my mum heard about it, and she and Dad were talking this morning."

"Why . . ." Penny's voice cracked. "Why did the police think Ralph is a vandal?"

"Because he *is*!" Tish said, looking puzzled.

"I know," Penny said, "but how did the *police* know?"

"Oh," Tish said. "My mum said that her friend said that someone *saw* Ralph and his gang, smashing a pay phone. And reported them." She peered at Penny. "Are you all right?"

Penny was a long way from all right. She felt chilled and weak and shaky, as if she was coming down with the flu. But it wasn't an illness that was troubling her. It was fear.

She guessed that Ralph and the vandalized telephone must have been reported by the tall man who had come along when she had been facing Ralph and his gang. But she was sure that Ralph wouldn't believe that.

Ralph would think that *she* had reported them.

And he and his gang would carry out their threat to *get* her if she said anything.

So much for Alan's advice, she thought miserably. Only being *warned* by the police wouldn't stop Ralph. The police might catch Ralph and punish him after he had taken revenge on her—but that would be too late to help her.

She thought about turning around and going home, pretending to be ill. But she didn't really want to spend the day alone in the house with her fear and misery. So she went off with Tish to school. But first she explained to her friend why she was so upset by the news about Ralph and the police.

"That's terrible!" Tish said, looking shocked. "Of *course* that stupid Ralph will blame you!" Then she pursed her mouth, eyes flashing. "But never you mind! He won't dare do anything if you've got lots of *friends* around you!"

Heroically, she rallied some of their other girl-friends to Penny's aid. For the rest of the school day, outside the classroom, they all stayed close to Penny. They helped her watch out for Ralph and his gang, and generally tried to keep her spirits up.

But Penny remained shaky and fearful. She knew that the other girls couldn't really do much to help her if Ralph and his gang decided to attack. And the point was proved that very day, after school.

Penny and her cluster of friends left the building together—and found Ralph waiting for them. With him were Errol and Gummy and Tony—all looking angry and threatening.

"You forgot what I said," Ralph growled at Penny, as the group of girls shrank back. "What would happen if you told."

"I *didn't* tell," Penny said faintly. "It must have been that man who came along . . ."

"Don't give me that," Ralph snarled. "He didn't see nothin'. It was you. So we're gonna get you."

The girls shrank away farther. Then two teachers passed by, and paused to stare warningly at the group of glowering boys facing the group of pale and nervous girls. So Ralph and his gang turned away, with another threat or two, and Penny and her friends fled.

"Never you mind," Tish said to Penny firmly as they set off for home. "We'll look after you."

Tish was clearly seeing herself as a courageous heroine facing great danger for the sake of a friend. But Penny wasn't finding anything enjoyable or heroic in her situation. And she knew that Tish and the others couldn't go on being with her every moment. There would be times when the other girls would have to be other places, doing other things.

In fact some of the girls—not such close friends as Tish—were already looking less than keen to go on playing bodyguard.

"Maybe you should tell someone," one of the girls suggested. "The teachers—even the police."

Penny shook her head. There wasn't anything to tell, since nothing had happened to her yet. At most, Ralph would get another warning, which would just make him more bent on taking revenge on Penny.

"Maybe Ralph will get bored and forget about it before long," said another girl.

Most of the others seemed to agree with that. And the belief, or hope, clearly seemed to cheer them up. All except Penny. She knew that it would be the other girls who got bored and forgot about her, long before Ralph did.

So, because she knew she would have to be on her own sooner or later, she decided bleakly that it might as well be sooner, and get it over with. When the group came to the corner where she usually turned off, to go the rest of the way home by herself, she announced that she would do just that, as always.

Most of the girls looked relieved at not having to go any farther out of their way. But Tish frowned worriedly.

"You really oughtn't to go *any*where alone, after what Ralph said," she told Penny.

"He's not around here," Penny said, waving a hand at the quiet streets. "I'll be fine."

The others trailed away, with Tish looking back once or twice, still frowning. And Penny hurried toward her house, alone.

Though she had said she would be fine, she didn't *feel* fine. Her insides felt frozen again, and as if they were tying themselves in knots. Time and again she glanced around, certain that she could hear footsteps behind her. But there was no one.

At least there was no one behind her.

But when she was almost within sight of her house, she found that what she feared was in *front* of her.

She was on a short street with houses on only one side, tucked behind screens of hedges and small trees. On the other side was a site where a large development—several blocks of flats— was being built. It had been raining that afternoon and so the builders hadn't been working. The site was silent and empty behind the fence that guarded it—a high, solid fence made of rough boards, standing twice Penny's height.

As she walked alongside that fence, she saw a group of four come around the corner ahead of her.

Errol and Gummy and Tony. And, ahead of them, big Ralph—with an ugly grin on his face and his hands bunched into fists.

8

HOT PURSUIT

Penny turned and ran. Behind her she could hear yells and thudding feet as the four boys galloped after her. But Penny was a naturally fast runner, made even faster by panic. In a flash she had reached the corner and whisked around it, hardly slowing down for the turn.

The high wooden fence of the building site also continued around that corner, so it was still alongside Penny as she fled down the side street. She looked ahead, hoping desperately for an opening that she could duck through, to get out of sight. But the whole length of the fence was blank and unbroken. And on the other side of the street stood another terrace of small houses, with no lanes or passages offering escape.

For an instant Penny slowed her wild dash, and glanced back. The four boys hadn't yet come around the corner after her, and there was no one else in sight. So she took a deep breath, and used the only form of escape that was open to her.

Silently calling on the pendant in her mind, she took another stride forward—and leaped.

Again she had the feeling that had come over her before. As if she was riding an invisible lift, which raised her swiftly up and up into the air.

Smoothly, gloriously, Penny flew in a swooping curve up to the top of the high fence, and over.

This time the power didn't shut off, as it had so disastrously in the library. The pendant, for once, worked *perfectly*. She soared downward as smoothly as she had risen. Then the power placed her on the ground as lightly and delicately as the settling of an autumn leaf.

And deposited her into the middle of a broad, knee-deep, extremely muddy puddle of water.

She stood for several seconds without moving, feeling the cold sludgy water rippling around her legs, not sure whether she was going to laugh or cry. In the end she did neither, because of the need for silence. A burst of voices from the other side of the fence told her that Ralph and his gang had at last reached the spot where she had taken off into the air.

They were breathing hard and all talking at once. "Gone!" "She's *fast!*" "Where'd she go?" "Maybe she climbed the fence . . ."

Those last words made Penny hold her breath. But then came Ralph's voice, rough with fury.

"The *fence?* Could *you* climb that fence? Stupid berk—she's only a *girl!* Prob'ly hidin' somewhere . . . Spread out an' look!"

The clatter of feet told Penny that they were on the move again. The sounds faded as the gang ran off along the street. Soon all was silent.

Carefully, Penny waded out of the pool, squelching her way to a patch of dry ground. Her shoes and socks were sodden and thick with mud, and the hem of her good school skirt was dripping. She had a fair idea what her mother would say about all that. But more important just then was the need to find a way out of the building site.

She was unwilling to use the pendant again, to leap the fence. She had been desperate before, but now she had time to stop and think. She knew how lucky she had been that the magic had worked so well—and, also, that the building site was empty. If she flew *back* over the fence, the flight might go wrong somehow. And she wouldn't know what, or who, might be on the other side. She didn't want to fly down in front of astonished people. Or into the midst of Ralph and his gang.

After wandering around the site for a few minutes, she finally found an opening in the fence, with wide slatted gates. The gates were locked, but they were lower than the fence and had crosspieces on the inside. So Penny could scramble over them fairly easily, once she had made sure that Ralph and company were nowhere in sight.

During the scramble she managed to snag her pullover and rip the soggy hem of her skirt. So she arrived home looking more like a refugee than a schoolgirl. And her mother said most of the things that Penny expected—beginning with "PenELope!"

But at least, Penny thought to herself later, she had made a terrific escape from the four boys. In fact her main feeling that evening was delight, or perhaps triumph. She was feeling a lot less afraid of Ralph—because she was sure, now, that with the pendant she could protect herself.

After all, she thought, it had worked perfectly when it lifted her over the fence. It wasn't the pendant's fault that there had been a puddle. So maybe its magic wasn't as damaged as Glumdole had said. Maybe it was mostly all right, and she was getting better at using it.

She went to school the next day feeling much less troubled. She even blithely told Tish and the other girls that they needn't worry about her anymore.

"I'm not going to creep around being afraid of a lot of thugs," she said. "They won't get me. I can look after myself."

The girls looked puzzled and impressed, though Tish looked puzzled and worried. Still, they all seemed relieved that they wouldn't have to go on being bodyguards anymore.

That afternoon, after school, Penny went home alone. But she decided not to be *too* foolhardy, so she went by a different route from usual—circling a long way around, along streets that she normally never used.

Luckily for her, one or two of those streets had several shops. When something in a shop window made her stop and turn and look, she saw something else. Ralph and his three friends, marching grimly along some distance behind her.

They weren't charging at her, because there were several adults passing by. So Penny had time to make a getaway. She walked as quickly as she could out of the shopping area, then glanced back. The four boys were still after her—and were breaking into a run.

Once again Penny fled like a startled deer. She turned a corner into a quiet residential street and put on a tremendous burst of speed. She was aiming to get to the next corner before her pursuers came into view. But she didn't quite make it.

She was suddenly startled, and thrown off her stride, by an enormous black-and-tan dog. The beast wasn't just barking at her—it was raging like some enormous fanged monster from a bad dream. It was being kept back by a wire gate—part of the fence in front of the house where it lived—and Penny was amazed that the gate was strong enough to hold it.

But the fright from the dog had slowed her up just enough.

"There she is!" she heard someone yell. She turned to see Ralph and his thugs sprinting toward her.

Panic took hold of her, and she was about to leap away. But then the dog's wild roaring grew noisier—and an idea struck through Penny's panic and stopped her.

The four boys, in full charge, had nearly reached the gate where the dog was raging. Backing away, Penny made a careful picture in her mind of what she wanted to happen—and called on the pendant.

The gate didn't just open. With a great *sprong* of taut wire being released, it was ripped from its posts and flung across the front garden.

Roaring even louder, jaws gaping, the dog hurled itself out into the street. And no boys ever moved more swiftly than Ralph and his friends then moved.

Errol and Tony made amazing leaps that carried them together over the picket fence at the front of the house next door. Ralph took three giant steps that got him up on top of a parked van. And Gummy, for all his tubbiness, shinned up a slender oak tree with an agility that would have done credit to a monkey.

Holding in her laughter, Penny backed farther away. But the dog was no longer interested in her. For some reason it seemed most infuriated by Gummy. It leaped again and again up the tree trunk, slavering and roaring, teeth snapping inches below the tubby youth's bottom. Penny saw that the tree was beginning to bend a little under Gummy's weight, and the teeth were getting closer and closer to their target.

An old lady threw open a window in the house next door. "You get out of my garden!" she shrilled at Errol and Tony. "I'll call the police!"

At the same time, a man came out of a house

across the street. "Get off my van, you hooligan!" he roared at Ralph.

And still at the same time another man came out of the house where the dog belonged, called the dog to him, then bellowed at Gummy. "You'll pay for this gate, you vandals!"

The four boys all yelled back, which made the adults shout even more furiously. In the midst of the uproar, Penny quietly made her way home. In fits of giggles, most of the way.

She laughed to herself all that evening, and was still laughing the following morning. She was also feeling more confident—perhaps a bit *too* confident—that she and the pendant could deal with Ralph and his gang. With her fears mostly out of the way, she was ready to enjoy the day, which was Saturday.

Saturday afternoon was the time when Penny went to her regular music lesson. Her piano teacher lived almost all the way across town, so Penny had to take the bus. Along the way she kept a sharp lookout, but she saw no sign of Ralph and his gang. And after the music lesson, on her way home, again she saw no sign of the boys.

So she was feeling relaxed and happy as she got off the bus at the stop near her home.

Until she saw what was waiting for her.

Ralph and his three friends, glaring at her. And they were sitting on *bikes*.

Behind them was what looked to Penny like a small army. Nearly twenty boys from school, in a sort of half circle. Some were just staring at her, but others were grinning, eagerly and nastily.

And all of them, too, were on bikes.

9

HUNTERS ON WHEELS

Penny felt as if her shoes were glued to the pavement. Her knees turned watery, her spine turned icy, her heart tried to climb up into her throat. White-faced, wide-eyed, she stared back at the throng of boys.

Most of them saw the signs of terror on her face. And they laughed—cruel, horrible laughter.

"Won't get away this time!" Errol shouted.

"Run as fast as you like!" Tony yelled.

"No dogs here!" Gummy jeered.

Big Ralph merely grinned evilly, while behind him the crowd of boys laughed, and gripped their handlebars, and got ready.

Penny found that somehow her feet had become unstuck and had started moving, as if by themselves. The boys watched her backing away, laughed some more, but still did not charge. They knew she had no hope of outrunning some twenty bikes.

Oddly, in that moment, Penny was reminded of a film she had seen, where a number of posh people were shown gathering to go fox hunting. On the back street where she stood there were no horses and hounds, no shiny boots and bright jackets. But these schoolboys on bikes were wearing the same expression on their faces as the fox hunters.

It was an expression that was both smug and cruel at the same time. An expression worn by hunters who feel superior and clever and who *know* they are going to make their kill. Because they are large and numerous, while their quarry is small and alone.

Ralph was still grinning his evil grin. "You better *run,*" he told Penny. "We'll even give you a head start, count to ten. More fun that way. Go on—*run!*"

Penny ran. Gathering every ounce of speed, she fled away along the street, swung around the corner. Behind her she could hear excited shouts and laughter and the clatter of pedals as the hunters got their bikes under way. Tears stung

Penny's eyes, half blinding her. A sob rose in her throat that threatened to burst out into a wail.

They *didn't* count to ten, she thought wildly. The *cheats!*

Somehow the fact that they hadn't given her a head start, after all, had a strange effect on her. She began to feel less frantic, less panicky. Her tears dried. She was still afraid, still running at top speed—but at the same time she had begun to feel deeply, fiercely *angry*.

From the sounds of the shouting and laughter behind her, she could tell that the boys weren't chasing her very rapidly. That made her angrier—that they didn't think they had to hurry, that they thought they could catch her with ease. And the thought of how many there were, the sheer unfairness, made her angrier still.

She guessed that Ralph and his three friends had gathered their troop of hunters with some kind of mixture of threats and promises. But the other boys hadn't looked *unwilling* to take part in the hunt. They had all looked as if they were enjoying themselves.

So fury wrapped itself around Penny, as she sped along the street. Behind her, the yelling group of boys turned the corner, storming along after her, their bikes gathering speed. But by then Penny had reached the next corner, and flashed around it. Once again, in that moment, out of sight of her pursuers, she called on the pendant to lift her up.

If anyone had been watching, it would have looked like an Olympic gold-medal high jump. But it wasn't quite high enough.

Penny had been aiming to leap magically over the nearest hedge—a very tall, thick, tangled hedge that was badly in need of a trim. But this time the pendant's uplift went wrong.

It dropped her right into the middle of the hedge, in a tangle of threshing arms and legs and sharp twigs that clawed at her skin and clothing.

She had the sense to stop threshing, though, as the crowd of boys whizzed past her. Then she fought her way out of the hedge, trying to ignore the painful scratches, and dashed away.

But now she was going in a different direction following a route the hunters wouldn't expect. She was planning again to go the long way around, in a wide circle, and try to sneak past the gang.

She slowed her pace to a trot, to save her strength. But she was already panting hard from that first wild dash. If she didn't make her escape fairly soon, she thought, the gang would catch her simply because she wouldn't be able to run anymore.

"There she is!"

The yell jerked her head around. Four boys on bikes had swung into the street behind her. Ralph had somehow realized that they had passed by her. So, like a good commander, he had sent his force ranging out in small groups, through the nearby streets, to look for her.

For an instant panic swept over her again, for she could see no escape route. Then the unfairness of it all struck her once more—and panic was shoved aside by the return of her blazing anger.

And this time the anger made her realize something very important. She didn't need to use the pendant merely to escape.

She could strike back.

The four boys who had spotted her were still a few houses away when she turned to face them. They hooted with cruel joy, seeing their prey apparently giving up, and pedaled swiftly toward her.

Penny sent the pendant's magic reaching out to the bicycle of the boy in front, and the boy's nasty grin turned to a look of shock. Suddenly the brakes on his front wheel clamped on tight. The bike slid to an abrupt stop, nearly spilling its rider over the handlebars.

Then the two bikes just behind, unable to brake in time, crashed into the bike that had stopped. All three riders tumbled, yelling, to the pavement. And the fourth boy, who had been some way back, came to a skidding halt just in time—and sat staring open-mouthed at his three friends, lying in a tangled and groaning heap.

It had all happened in a few seconds, so quickly that Penny could hardly believe her eyes. But then she smiled an angry smile. That'll teach you, she thought, as she turned and trotted lightly away.

For a short while she moved unseen, with no sign of pursuit. She was still making the very wide circle that she hoped would take her around the remaining boys and finally get her home. But her anger was starting to fade, giving way to nervousness with every step.

At last she decided that it might be wiser to find a good, safe hiding place, and wait until it began to get dark. Then it would be easier to make her way home without being spotted.

She firmly put out of her mind what her mother would say *this* time, when she came home all sweaty and dirty, her clothes and skin torn by the hedge, and very late. She had enough to worry about, she told herself, trying to get home at all.

She jogged away, around another corner or

two, to where some playing fields led to a pleasant little park. The park had a number of paths for peaceful strolling, among the trees and grass. It also had pretty flower beds, some small ornamental pools and a great many dense thickets of shrubs and bushes—including broad screening tangles of rhododendron.

Once tucked into a thicket, Penny felt, she would never be discovered.

The playing fields were mostly deserted as she crossed them. She trotted down a grassy slope into the park. There she chose a likely-looking thicket to be her hiding place, and set off for it.

When she reached it, she saw that it was in fact just a thin screen of bushes beside one of the murky-looking ornamental pools. She glanced around, looking for another thicket—and stopped, with a gasp, heart fluttering.

All by himself, looking like some kind of avenging demon on wheels, big Ralph was flying down the slope on his bicycle.

He was heading directly for her, as if he intended to ride her down. His eyes were narrowed and glittering, his teeth showed in a vicious grin of triumph. Penny jumped aside, out of the path of the onrushing bike. And before Ralph could swing around toward her again, she hurled the pendant's magic at him.

The pendant twisted the front wheel of Ralph's bike sharply to one side, away from Penny.

The sharp turn didn't make Ralph fall off. He and the bike flashed away, with Ralph still bent over the handlebars but no longer pedaling. Penny had just a glimpse of his face, eyes wide and mouth gaping in an expression of total disbelief.

Then he made a noise that might have started as a yell but came out as a whimper.

And the bike went over the edge of the bank as if off a ski jump, sailed gracefully through the air, and fell with a glorious splash into the middle of the ornamental pool.

10

PERILOUS FLIGHT

If this was a story, Penny thought, it'd be all over now, and I would have won.

But it wasn't over, and she hadn't won. Even dropping Ralph in the pool had only made him more furious and determined. So, much later, more than two hours after Ralph's dip, Penny was still no closer to getting home.

During those two hours, also, she had been through more wild pursuits and escapes. And in each of those adventures she had saved herself with the pendant—though never in the way she had planned.

The first time had been soon after she had dashed out of the park, while Ralph was still splashing his way back to dry land. A group of boys had spotted her and had given chase, whooping and yelling. And again, Penny had struck back.

A pile of plastic sacks, bulging with rubbish, was heaped high at the side of the street, waiting to be collected. Without stopping to think, Penny took hold of the sacks with the pendant's magic and flung them into the street, to block the path of the bikes.

But the pendant overdid it. As the sacks flew up into the air, they were torn open. A flood of messy, soggy, stinking rubbish gushed out from the sacks, all over the horrified boys.

Penny hadn't waited around to see what happened. But from the shrieks and clangs that she heard behind her, she had been sure none of those boys would be coming after her.

Another adventure took place some while later, some streets farther on. Penny had then been spotted by two of Ralph's close followers, lanky Errol and stocky Tony. As they yelled and rode full tilt toward her, Penny dashed into a nearby front garden, with a thick hedge around it. But then she saw that there was no other way out—that she was trapped.

Errol and Tony were riding hard toward the open gate of the garden when Penny struck out with the pendant's power. A garden hose, coiled on the grass beside her, rose up like a hissing

serpent. Icy water gushed from its nozzle—and struck both boys full in the face.

It then swung around and drenched Penny too, but she hardly noticed. She was enjoying watching the two boys. Shrieking, unable to see for a moment, they missed the open gate of the garden and rode their bikes headlong into the depths of the hedge.

Now *you* know what prickly hedges feel like, Penny thought, as she ran off.

During those hectic hours Penny had begun to feel slightly worried about what she was doing. She was worrying especially about two things— apart from her main worry, which was about how to get home.

First, she was worried that the pendant's magic might go *so* wrong, sometime, that some of the hunters might get seriously hurt or even killed. So far all the boys had been lucky, suffering only cuts and bruises and hurt pride. But Penny knew that their injuries could have been worse, because there was no telling what the pendant might do at any time. And no matter how angry she was, she didn't want to do any *serious* damage to anyone. Not even to Ralph.

The second thing worrying her was that she had been performing some quite startling magic. Surely the pursuing boys would be asking questions about the amazing crashing bikes, flying rubbish bags, and hoses that seemed to come alive? If such weird things kept happening, someone sometime might make the right guesses about the *cause*. And then the secret of the pendant might be revealed.

So, as she jogged along, Penny decided that she would try not to use the pendant anymore, certainly not to go on striking back. Instead, she would simply get home as quickly as she could.

Also, a glance at her watch showed that it was getting late. The afternoon shadows had been growing longer and longer. Now the shadows were joining together and darkening, as twilight began to fall. Which would make it even easier, Penny thought, to sneak past the remaining boys and get home.

By then she was coming close to the end of the long, roundabout route that she had been following. Home was only a short distance away. She speeded up a little—until she heard the voices. And saw the four figures, clustered in a patch of shadow under a tree, ahead of her.

She shrank back into some shadows of her own, her heart beating fast. But they hadn't seen her, so she relaxed a little and began thinking about what to do.

She had come to a broad churchyard, which had a tall fence of upright, wrought iron railings around it. She knew that the *far* side of the churchyard was very near to her house. But the four shadowy figures were in her way.

She didn't want to set out on another round-about route—and she didn't think she needed to. If she could sneak *into* the churchyard, and get across it and out again, she could get safely home without being seen.

She crept forward quietly, screened by a few bushes growing along the iron fence. The group of four, ahead, were muttering quietly to one another and didn't look her way. Two more steps brought her, as she expected, to a narrow gate in the fence. She glanced up at the railings, towering high above her head. Then, hardly daring to breathe, she pushed gently at the gate.

She nearly moaned aloud with relief as the gate swung open with only the tiniest of creaks.

Quickly she slid into the churchyard, ducking behind a large tree. There she found that she was closer to the four shadowy figures, and could hear them clearly.

It was Ralph and his three main followers, as she expected. Leaning against the tree, she listened.

". . . just us now," she heard Errol saying. "The others 've all gone home."

"Babies," Ralph said harshly. "Gone home to mum."

"A lot of them got bashed up," Gummy said. "All those accidents . . . It was *weird* . . ."

"Never mind about accidents!" Ralph snarled.

Penny grinned to herself, wondering how wet Ralph still might be.

"But it was *weird*!" Gummy repeated. "Like when that dog got out . . . Only t'day it was rubbish bags flyin' around . . . and everybody's bikes sort of goin' crazy . . . *ow*!"

The very last sound was because Ralph had cuffed Gummy sharply on the head. "Stop goin' *on* about it, I told you!" Ralph snapped. "People have accidents all the time! 'Specially if they're chasin' someone, ridin' fast, takin' chances . . . I don't want to *hear* all that other stuff! Right?"

"Right," Errol said. "All those weird stories, that's those other kids makin' things up so they could give up an' go home."

"Or maybe they were seein' things," Tony said, "after crashin' their bikes an' hittin' their heads."

"Right," Errol said.

"*Right*," Ralph said warningly.

"Oh, right, right," Gummy said quickly.

Penny smiled to herself again. It was like Glumdole said, she thought. People just don't believe in magic anymore. They can't imagine that it could be possible. And so they refuse to

85

believe that a magical thing could happen even when it has just happened to *them*.

It was an interesting fact, she thought. And useful, for her. It meant that if anyone else ever accidentally saw her doing something magical with the pendant, they would refuse to believe their own eyes.

She was thinking about that, no longer listening closely to the boys, when what Ralph was saying caught her attention and wiped the smile from her face.

". . . so we go to her house," Ralph was saying. "Maybe she got past those other berks an' already got home. But if not, we find places to hide, an' wait. An' grab her when she gets there."

Behind her tree Penny went tense. She was going to have to hurry, to get home before the four boys found their hiding places near her house. And if the gate on the *far* side of the churchyard was locked, she would have to get over the fence . . . another way.

She moved away from the tree, crouching, trying to be catlike. The twilight was even deeper by then—and a light drizzle had begun to fall. That was another reason for hurrying. So was the fact that while she had often been in the churchyard before, the darkening shadows were making it very spooky.

But she hurried a little too quickly.

A tangle of long wet grass clutched at her foot, and she stumbled. Her other foot skidded on wet stone, and she fell—with a thump and a gasp. And that was the moment when the gate that she had opened, being properly balanced on its hinges, swung itself shut—with an echoing clang.

"There—in the graveyard!" Errol said.

"It's *her!*" Ralph shouted.

Their feet thundered on the pavement as they dashed toward the gate that Penny had used.

She sprang up, once again a hunted animal. A panicky sprint brought her to the huge dark bulk of the church itself, before the four boys were inside the churchyard. But she could hear them pounding along after her.

Without slowing, Penny fled around the church. That brought her to the far side of the churchyard, to the fence where she knew another gate stood. Breathlessly she flung herself against the gate's chill iron uprights.

It clanked, but didn't open. Some caretaker had at least remembered to lock *this* gate.

Penny glanced back. She could hear the boys, but they hadn't yet come around the church.

"All right, pendant," she breathed desperately. "Come *on!*"

The magic responded. Penny was thrust into the air by the invisible lift. Up she went, with the ugly spear-points of the gate's iron railings flashing past her.

But the pendant didn't sweep her down to the ground on the other side of the fence. Nor did the power shut off.

Up and up she went, flung higher and higher by the magic lifting that would not stop. She could only scream a soundless scream as she was whirled dizzyingly up—high above the trees, high enough to look down on rooftops, high enough to make her eyes blur with terror.

Then the power swung her to one side. As she fought to draw the breath she needed for a shriek, she felt her legs bump painfully against something hard. She blinked her blurred eyes and saw a weird metal shape that she dimly recognized as a rusty old weather vane, standing on the very top of a large pointed thing . . .

That was when the pendant's power cut off— and dropped her.

She just had time to fling her arms around the base of the weather vane. It groaned, but held. And there she sprawled, full length, hanging desperately from the vane.

Hanging down along the steep, rain-slippery slope of the terrifyingly high spire that was at the very top of the church steeple.

11

ONLY ONE WAY DOWN

Blind panic stormed through Penny like a hurricane. She seemed unable to see or feel or think, to know who she was or where she was. Her terror was so total that she might have fainted. And then she would have lost her grip on the weather vane, would have fallen all the long way down from the spire.

But through the panic she began to hear something. Strange voices, as if out of a dream, from far away. Not the voices of friends, nor of someone trying to help her—but angry, threatening voices.

"Where'd she *go*?" one voice was raging. "She didn't fly away, did she? *Look* for her!"

"Maybe she got inside somehow," another distant voice said.

"Right," said the first, angriest voice. "Let's go look!"

Hearing those faraway sounds had a healing effect on Penny. She started to come out of the total panic, to get her mind working again. Some part of her mind told her that the voices had been those of Ralph and Errol, searching for her far below. That part of her mind also reminded her that she had good reason to be afraid of the owners of the voices.

It seemed a silly, puny fear compared to the terror she felt then, clinging to the weather vane. But the very silliness of it somehow prodded the rest of her mind back into action. Including what crumbs were left of her courage.

Slowly her eyes began to focus and her breathing grew easier. Fighting hard against the panic that kept trying to take over again, she tried to think what to do. She tightened her grip on the vane, twisted her head around a little, and looked down.

The sight made her shudder, and the vane groaned again, faintly, where she clutched it. She had seen how high up she was, and how helpless she was.

There was no way that she could move. The slope of the spire was far too steep—almost straight up. She could not possibly have clung on to that slope, to climb down, even if the steeple had been completely dry. As it was, wet and slippery with rain, she had less chance. If she let go of the vane she would simply slide off the steeple and fall.

Far below her, she heard a muffled crash. It sounded like a heavy door slamming—which told her that Ralph and the others had gone into the church to look for her. At least, if they were inside, she thought, they were out of the way. It didn't occur to her for a moment that she might call out to them, when they came out. She felt sure that they wouldn't help her even if they could. They would probably just go away, laughing, and leave her.

And calling to someone else for help was probably also hopeless. For one thing, the streets around the churchyard were as empty as a smallish town's streets can be at twilight. Besides, she doubted that anyone passing would hear her if she called. Or would know where her cries were coming from. Who would think to look for a frightened girl on top of a church spire?

So, she thought fearfully, even if I scream no one is likely to come. Not soon enough, anyway. She could already feel her grip weakening on the weather vane, as her hands and arms grew tired.

In a little while her strength would give out altogether . . .

Again she fought against a surge of panic. There was only one way down for her, she knew. Yet the thought of it was nearly as terrifying as the thought of staying there. The pendant . . .

But the magic had gone more seriously wrong than ever before, this time. She didn't think that she could trust it to get her down. It might lift her up even higher, and away from the steeple, and then drop her. It might take her up and up and never stop. It might do anything. She simply couldn't quite find the nerve to risk it.

She fought against the panic again, fought against a storm of sobbing, fought the tears that spilled down her cheeks. And as she fought, with wavering courage and fading strength, a tiny nudge came out of her memory. A nudge that reminded her of one thing she hadn't thought of, one place where she might get help.

She raised her tear-streaked, rain-wet face. Every scrap of her terror and desperation burst out in a piercing, drawn-out scream that stabbed up into the evening sky.

"*GLUMDO-O-O-LE!*"

"Really," said a breathy, high-pitched voice above her head. "You could just say my name quietly, you know. When people have a name-tie, there's no need to *shout*."

Penny lifted her head higher, looking up. The cobold was perched calmly on the south arm of the weather vane, wearing the same cloak and hood, looking at her with the same frown.

"Glumdole," Penny whispered. The relief that poured through her was so total that she almost relaxed her grip on the vane.

Glumdole sighed sorrowfully. "You humans. What messes you get into, playing with magic. I suppose you've been trying to *fly*. People always want to do that. Even with a broken pendant . . ."

"Glumdole . . ." Penny said again, weakly.

"Of course it wouldn't be *true* flying, not even if the pendant was working properly," Glumdole went on gloomily. "Not flying around, hither and yon, like a bird. The pendant just lifts you up . . ."

"*Glum*dole," Penny said, a little more loudly.

". . . and sets you down again." Glumdole frowned down at her. "Were you saying something?"

"Please," Penny said wretchedly. "Get me down."

Glumdole blinked. "Down? Oh. Ah. Yes. You *do* look a little uncomfortable. Didn't you intend to be up here?"

"Glumdole!" Penny wailed. *"Down!"*

"Yes, yes," Glumdole said, sounding put out. "Always in a *rush,* humans."

He lifted a finger, then waggled a pointed ear. As he did so, he rose in the air, still in a sitting position. Then Penny felt as if invisible, gentle hands were taking hold of her and lifting her as well. Her hands slid away from the weather vane. For an instant she hung in midair, face-to-face with Glumdole's frown. Then Glumdole blinked, and waggled the other ear.

And they were standing on the ground, just in front of the church doors.

Penny stumbled, her legs rubbery, and might have fallen if Glumdole hadn't gripped her arm with a narrow, strong hand. He peered closely at her, frowning.

"You shouldn't really go up on steeples," he told her, "if you have no head for heights."

"I didn't . . ." Penny began, then stopped. She had heard a thump and a crash and a shout from inside the church, where the four boys were still searching for her.

"Glumdole," she said shakily, "inside the church there are some boys who've been . . . trying to hurt me. Could you find some way to *keep* them in there?"

Glumdole frowned so deeply that his eyes nearly disappeared among the wrinkles. "Trying to *hurt* you, Penelope? Why, there's a great many things I might do to them! I could send them to a dragon I know, who would quite like . . ."

"No, no," Penny interrupted. "Just keep them in the church. Please. Then when I get home I can call the police . . ."

Glumdole's frown cleared a little. He looked at the church, twitching an eyebrow. Penny could hear strange little clicks and squeaks coming from all around the building.

"There," Glumdole said. "The doors won't open now, and I've put a can't-be-broken spell on the windows. Quite nice stained glass . . ."

"Thank you," Penny said. Then, as she realized that all the terrors of the long afternoon and evening were finally at an end, she suddenly felt weak and dizzy. She swayed, barely feeling Glumdole's hands grip her arms again. And his voice sounded hollow and faraway, so that she could barely understand him.

"It's all right, Penelope," he was saying, very gently. "I understand now what must have happened here. But it's all right. Glumdole will fix it. Everything will be fine."

And the last thing that Penny saw before she fainted was the tip of one of his pointed ears, waggling.

12

SAFEKEEPING

She awoke slowly, as if drifting up from the depths of a shadowed pool to the softly lit surface. When she opened her eyes, she remained still—enjoying the feeling of being comfortable, cozily warm, relaxed. She was in her own room, lying on her bed, and it felt much nicer than shivering in a rain-soaked churchyard.

But then she came fully awake, with a jolt, as the memory of the churchyard—and the steeple, and Glumdole, and all of it—flooded back into her mind. Glancing at her watch, she was jolted again to find that only half an hour had passed since she had first entered the churchyard, trying to bypass Ralph and the others.

Only thirty minutes, she thought numbly, get-

97

ting to her feet. Yet I'm home, I'm all dry, and I'm . . .

The third jolt came when she saw herself in the mirror. She didn't look anything like a girl who had been chased over half the town, scraped and scratched and soaked and bruised. Her clothes were as clean and neat as when she had put them on that morning. There were no scratches on her skin from the hedge, nor even a hair out of place. And she *felt* well—as if she had had a long, refreshing sleep.

Some people might then have wondered if they had dreamed the whole thing. But Penny knew better. The pendant still hung comfortably inside her pullover, and she was absolutely certain that other sorts of magic had been happening in her room, tidying her up.

"Glumdole?" she whispered.

But she was alone in her room, and remained alone. That made her uneasy, since she remembered Glumdole telling her that she didn't need to shout to call him. Maybe something was wrong . . .

"Glumdole?" she said again, a bit more loudly.

With an almost soundless *pop,* the cobold appeared—perched on the edge of her dresser.

"Sorry to be slow," he said. "I was at the church, watching to be sure that the constables were in position before I removed the spells and freed the church doors."

Penny blinked. "Constables? You mean the *police* are at the church?"

"Indeed," Glumdole said. "You had said that you wanted to alert them, but you were . . . asleep." He sighed. "So I made the call that you would have made. It isn't difficult to use a telephone, or to make myself sound like a law-abiding human reporting a crime."

Penny giggled. So, she thought, Ralph and the other three would have been caught in the act, apparently vandalizing the church. Now they would get what they deserved—and they would no longer be in a position to do anything to her.

"I left the can't-be-broken spell on the church windows, though," Glumdole went on. "It really is *excellent* stained glass."

Penny smiled at him with affection. "That's nice. You've really been very kind—bringing me here, cleaning me up . . . I'm ever so grateful."

Glumdole shifted on the dresser as if embarrassed. "No need, no need. The least I could do. Especially after you got into such trouble on the steeple, because of the pendant. I feel . . . responsible."

"Oh, you mustn't!" Penny said quickly "The

pendant just went wrong, like it usually does. It's nobody's fault!"

Glumdole sighed deeply. "Yet I am its maker. And I feel now, even more strongly, Penelope, that you should let me also be its destroyer. Before it brings even more harm and disaster down upon you."

Penny raised one hand to the pendant protectively.

"Remember, Penelope," Glumdole added, "you can never know what the pendant may do. You may not always have time to call upon me for help, before you are hurt or even killed."

"I know," Penny said in a small voice. "But today the pendant also *saved* me, from Ralph and his gang."

Glumdole sighed heavily. "No doubt. But you must understand the dangers . . ."

"Oh, I *do!*" Penny said. "But maybe, with more practice, I could sort of get the *hang* of it better!"

Glumdole frowned his gloomiest frown. "I doubt that very much. But I can see that you are determined to keep the thing. And I cannot forbid you, for it is yours." He shook his head sadly. "I shall simply beg you to use it *responsibly,* Penelope. *Think* before wielding the magic. Be *cautious,* Penelope—as much as you can in your impulsive youth."

Penny looked into the cobold's eyes, saw the fondness and the concern for her that was there. "I'll try, Glumdole," she said softly.

"You might even decide not to wear it all the time," Glumdole added. "So you won't be tempted to use it unnecessarily."

Penny nodded. "All right. I'll put it away, some of the time. Maybe most of the time. Don't worry, Glumdole. It'll be all right."

"I hope so . . ." Glumdole began.

But then his voice cut off—because he was no longer there.

As Penny blinked at the empty air where he had been sitting, the door to her room crashed open.

"*Here* you are!" said her brother Alan loudly. "And talking to yourself! First sign of insanity, that is!"

And he laughed uproariously, so that the bottle of cola in his hand jiggled and splashed a little.

Penny whirled, glaring at him. "I've told you *never* to come in here without knocking!" she said furiously. "You can't—"

But Alan ignored her, raising his voice to talk over top of her words. "What're you doing, anyway, sneaking in without saying anything. Mum's really worried, thinking you're not home yet. Why don't you come downstairs?"

With an infuriating grin, he turned away. As

he did so, he raised the bottle to his lips. That was when Penny's anger boiled over.

So did Alan's drink, as she flung the pendant's magic at it.

Fizzing and foaming, the cola erupted from the neck of the bottle. It jetted straight into Alan's astonished face, gushing and splashing down to drench the front of his shirt.

"Aghhh!" Alan shouted, almost dropping the bottle as he pawed frantically at his dripping shirt.

"That will teach you," Penny told him sweetly, "not to go jumping around, bursting into people's rooms."

And she pushed him through the door, and closed it firmly behind him.

Then she stood still, gazing thoughtfully at the place on her dresser where Glumdole had been sitting. Trying hard to stop smiling as she remembered the look on Alan's face as the cola squirted unnaturally into it, she thought of what the cobold had said. I suppose I shouldn't have done that to Alan, she said to herself. Something might have gone wrong, and he could have been hurt . . .

Glumdole was right, she told herself sternly. It *is* dangerous. I should take the pendant off and *leave* it off—so I don't use it stupidly, without thinking.

Slowly, as if her hands were unwilling to obey her, she pulled the pendant's chain up over her head. Then she looked around the room. What I should do, she thought, is put it somewhere safe. Lock it away, so it's really hard for me to get at. So I won't be *tempted*, like Glumdole said, and get into more trouble on another steeple or something.

But as she stood there with the pendant in her hand, she realized that the memory of her terror on the steeple was already beginning to fade. And, also, that other thoughts were crowding into her mind. Thoughts of what she had done, with rubbish sacks and garden hoses and so on, to the boys who had chased her—and who deserved everything that had happened to them. But also thoughts of how she might just as easily, other times, do *nice* things with her magic— for nice people, who would deserve such things.

She caught sight of herself in the mirror—and saw the smile curving her lips, the gleam in her eyes. Stooping swiftly, she opened the bottom drawer of her dresser and tucked the pendant in at the back.

No sense making the pendant too hard to get at, she told herself.

There's no knowing when I might want it again.